I Want a Dinosaur!

An Ivy and Mack story

Contents

Written by Jane Clarke

Illustrated by Gustavo Mazali

with Adrienn Greta Schönberg

Collins

What's in this story?

Listen and say

dinosaurs

Triceratops

Tyrannosaurus Rex (T-Rex)

Pterodactyl

Microraptor

Ankylosaurus

Diplodocus

Stegosaurus

Chapter 1 We can't wait!

Grandpa showed Mack and Ivy his old book about dinosaurs.

"I learned all about dinosaurs from this book." he said.

"I love dinosaurs!" said Mack.

"Me, too!" said Ivy.

Grandpa looked on his computer. "There are dinosaurs at the **museum**!" he said. "Would you like to go?"

"Yes, please!" said Ivy.

"I want to meet a dinosaur!" said Mack.

Grandpa bought three tickets for *Meet the Dinosaurs*.

The museum had a lot of big rooms, a shop, and a café. When they got there, they looked at the map.

"Where are the dinosaurs?" asked Grandpa.

Ivy pointed to a **huge** hall.

"I can't **wait** to meet a dinosaur!" said Mack.

MEET THE DINOSAURS

There was a long line of people. They waited to go **inside**.

"Waiting is **boring**," said Mack.

"I **hate** waiting," said Ivy.

"I hate waiting, too," said Grandpa.

"My favorite dinosaur is T-Rex," Mack told Grandpa and Ivy. "It had huge teeth and **claws** and it made a big noise, *raar!*"

Everyone jumped.

"My favorite dinosaur is a Diplodocus," said Ivy.

"*Stomp, stomp, stomp!*"

"*My* favorite dinosaur is a very small, quiet one," Grandpa said, with a smile.

They went inside. "Wow," said Ivy. "These are big eggs!"

"Dinosaurs came out of eggs and so do crocodiles!" said Mack. "Crocodiles lived **at the time of** the dinosaurs!"

"I know that," said Ivy.

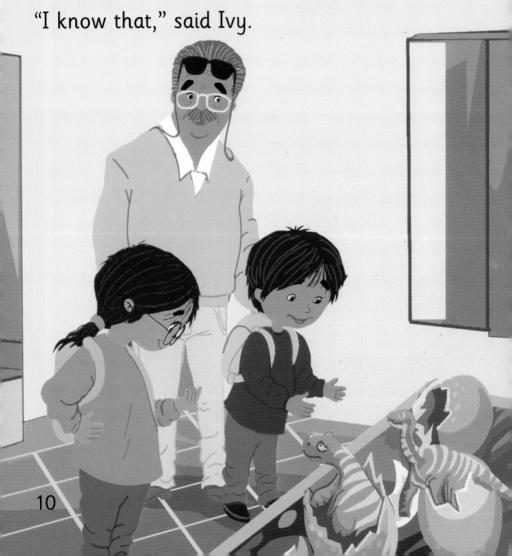

"Let's watch the dinosaur egg **hatch**!" said Mack. "A baby dinosaur is coming out!"

"There aren't any **real** dinosaur eggs," said Ivy, "or dinosaurs. They're all **fossils** now."

"I know that," said Mack. "Dinosaurs are very, very, very old." He laughed. "They're older than Grandpa!"

"I'm not old!" said Grandpa.

"This dinosaur is called an Ankylosaurus," said Ivy. "It ate plants and had a very strong tail."

"I know that!" said Mack.

"This dinosaur is called a Stegosaurus," said Mack. "It ate plants, too."

"I know that!" said Ivy.

"You two know a lot about dinosaurs," said Grandpa. "But do you know what this dinosaur is called? It always tried very hard to do something."

"Yes! A try, try, Try -ceratops!" said Mack and Ivy.

They all laughed.

Grandpa pointed up the stairs.

"Let's go up here!" he said. "I can see my favorite dinosaur!"

"That's a pterodactyl," said Mack. "Pterodactyls aren't dinosaurs."

"*We* know that," said Ivy. "But Grandpa doesn't."

Grandpa looked at the Pterodactyl. His **sunglasses** fell off his head. They fell onto the Pterodactyl. He couldn't get them back.

"It has my sunglasses," said Grandpa. "That *isn't* my favorite dinosaur."

Ivy hid behind a Diplodocus and waited. When she saw Mack and Grandpa, she jumped out at them.

They all laughed.

"This is *my* favorite dinosaur," Ivy told them.

Mack and Ivy stood next to the huge leg **bone**.

"Banjo the dog would like this bone!"
said Mack.

"Banjo eats dog biscuits," said Ivy.

Mack laughed. "A dinosaur would like dog
biscuits," he said.

"Only very big ones!" said Ivy.

Mack hid behind a T-Rex and waited. When he saw Ivy and Grandpa, he jumped out at them.

"Meet *my* favorite dinosaur," he said. "It was called Tyrannosaurus Rex. That means *The Lizard* **King**!"

"Hi, King T-Rex," Grandpa said. "I don't like your teeth."

Raar!

MEET THE
TYRANNOSAU
REX

"Its teeth are a lot bigger than crocodile teeth!" said Mack.

"I wouldn't like to meet a real T-Rex," said Ivy.

"I would!" said Mack.

19

There was a very loud noise in the next room.

Everyone jumped.

"What is that?" said Grandpa.

"Was that you, Mack?" said Ivy.

"It wasn't me," said Mack.

RAAR!

"Let's go and find out what it is," said Ivy.

"Wait for me!" said Grandpa.

There was a very, very, big T-Rex in the room. It looked at Mack. It moved its arms up and down and opened its huge mouth. Its big long teeth were very **close** to Mack's head.

RAAAAAARR!

"Watch out, Mack." Ivy **shouted**. "It's real!"

"It wants to eat me!" said Mack, and he ran out of the room.

Ivy and Grandpa ran after him.

Mack was in the next room. Ivy and Grandpa were very happy to see him.

"There you are, Mack," said Ivy.

"I waited for you," said Mack.

"Were you scared?" asked Grandpa.

"No!" said Mack.

Mack looked at the dinosaur fossil.

"You know that dinosaur isn't real, Mack. There aren't any dinosaurs now," said Ivy.

Mack looked at Ivy. "I think you're wrong, Ivy!" he said.

MEET THE MICRORAPTOR

25

Chapter 5 Birds are dinosaurs!

"This dinosaur is called a Microraptor," said Mack. "It was very small!"

"I like that dinosaur!" said Grandpa. "It's my favorite!"

"There are real dinosaurs now!" said Mack. "Birds are dinosaurs! They are part of the Microraptor family."

"I didn't know that!" said Ivy.

"So I have dinosaurs in my yard!" said Grandpa. "We can go home and meet *them*!"

Meet the NEW dinosaurs

Mack, Ivy, and Grandpa watched the birds in Grandpa's yard.

"The museum was fun," Ivy said.
"Thank you, Grandpa!"

"It was great to meet the dinosaurs!" said Mack.

"And now I know there are real dinosaurs in my yard!" said Grandpa.

"Ivy, do you want to go out into the yard and meet one?" Mack asked.

"We can try," said Ivy. "But they always fly away!"

Mini-dictionary

Listen and read

at the time of (phrase) If something happened **at the time of** something else, it happened at the same time in the past.

bone (noun) A **bone** is one of the hard white parts inside your body.

boring (adjective) Something that is **boring** is not very interesting or exciting.

claw (noun) An animal's **claws** are the hard nails at the end of its feet.

close (adjective) If something is **close** to something else, it is very near it.

fossil (noun) A **fossil** is the part of a plant or an animal that died a long time ago and has turned into rock.

hatch (verb) When an egg **hatches**, a baby bird or animal comes out of it.

hate (verb) If you **hate** someone or something, you don't like them at all.

huge (adjective) Something that is **huge** is very big.

inside (adverb) If you go **inside**, you go into a place.

king (noun) A **king** is a man from a royal family.

museum (noun) A **museum** is a place where you can look at interesting and important objects.

real (adjective) Something that is **real** is not a copy of that thing.

shout (verb) If you **shout**, you say something very loudly.

sunglasses (noun) **Sunglasses** are dark glasses that you wear to stop your eyes from hurting in the sun.

wait (verb) If you **wait**, you spend time in a place, usually doing nothing, before something happens.

1 Look and order the story

2 Listen and say

Collins

Published by Collins
An imprint of HarperCollins*Publishers*
Westerhill Road
Bishopbriggs
Glasgow
G64 2QT

HarperCollins*Publishers*
1st Floor, Watermarque Building
Ringsend Road
Dublin 4
Ireland

William Collins' dream of knowledge for all began with the publication of his first book in 1819.

A self-educated mill worker, he not only enriched millions of lives, but also founded a flourishing publishing house. Today, staying true to this spirit, Collins books are packed with inspiration, innovation, and practical expertise. They place you at the center of a world of possibility and give you exactly what you need to explore it.

ISBN 978-0-00-849041-6

Collins® and COBUILD® are registered trademarks of HarperCollins*Publishers* Limited

www.collins.co.uk/elt

British Library Cataloguing in Publication Data

A catalogue record for this publication is available from the British Library.

Author: Jane Clarke
Lead illustrator: Gustavo Mazali (Beehive)
Copy illustrator: Adrienn Greta Schönberg (Beehive)
Series editor: Rebecca Adlard
Publishing manager: Lisa Todd
Product managers: Jennifer Hall and Caroline Green
In-house editor: Alma Puts Keren
Project manager: Emily Hooton
Editors: Deborah Friedland and Samantha Lacey
Proofreaders: Natalie Murray and Michael Lamb
Cover designer: Kevin Robbins
Typesetter: 2Hoots Publishing Services Ltd
Audio produced by White House Sound Ltd
Reading guide author: Julie Penn
Production controller: Rachel Weaver
Printed and bound by: Pureprint Group, UK

Download the audio for this book and a reading guide for parents and teachers at www.collins.co.uk/peapoddownloads